Austin's PANSIES

Story by Phallon Perry

Illustrations by Ana Márquez

Inspiration

The character Austin is inspired by a young man named Austin, who is never afraid to go against the grain, even at a young age.

Dedication

Austin's Pansies is dedicated to the girls and boys of Baltimore, Maryland. There is beauty inside of you and all around you. Never forget that.

It was the weekend before Valentine's Day. On Saturday Austin and his parents cheered for his brother Bomani's basketball team and then they went to his sister Yessenia's softball practice.

Sunday was a normal Sunday. Austin went to church and prayed for the world to be happy and healthy. He even prayed about the snowflake ball. There were five days left until the school dance.

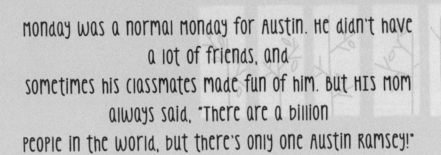

Monday was a normal Monday for Austin. He didn't have a lot of friends, and sometimes his classmates made fun of him. But HIS MOM always said, "There are a billion people in the world, but there's only one Austin Ramsey!"

Gina WAS Austin's neighbor and one of Austin's only friends. He could go to the snowflake ball by himself but wanted to go with her. Four more days until the ball.

Austin's mom was a florist and she always kept flowers around the house because flowers
help to keep the air clean. Austin's favorite flowers were the pansies that lived on his windowsill.

Tuesday was just a regular Tuesday. Austin watered his pansies and made sure that their leaves were healthy. There was Mr. and Mrs. Pansy, and their three children Ray Pansy, May Pansy and Eli Pansy. He talked to them every morning before school and every night before bed.

4

His big sister Yessenia was born in a country called Panama. On Tuesdays Austin's dad cooked a traditional Panamanian dinner to honor Yessenia's heritage but Austin was too nervous about the ball to finish his meal. Three days until the dance.

5

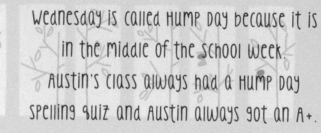

Wednesday is called HUMP Day because it is in the middle of the school week. Austin's class always had a HUMP Day spelling quiz and Austin always got an A+.

During their walk home from school Gina sneezed five times! The Ball was in two days and Austin was worried that Gina would be too sick to go!

6

Austin sat near his pansies and prayed for Gina to be okay.

That night his pansies came to life. Austin took such good care of his flowers, his flowers wanted to take care of him too.

7

The next morning Austin's mom woke him up, he ran to his window to see if Gina was awake. She was still asleep.

Austin threw a few pebbles at Gina's window to wake her up. "What's wrong Austin?" Gina asked. "Why aren't you getting dressed for school? Austin asked. "I have winter allergies, that's why I was sneezing so much yesterday. No school for me today. My mom says I should rest. See you later!"

Thursday mornings were always special. Thursdays Austin's family celebrated his older brother Bomani's heritage. He was born in Malawi and Austin's dad loved making the family a traditional Malawian breakfast before school.

Only one day left until Valentine's Day and things were not looking good for Austin. In art class everyone made decorations for the ball, but Austin made a get well soon card for Gina. And to top things off, Austin received a **C** on his spelling quiz!

When he got home from school Austin did his homework and sat by his windowsill and told the pansies all about his day. Once Austin went to sleep, the pansies came up with a plan.

Pansies love Valentine's Day. Cupid liked pansy flowers because they represent love. Cupid would pick pansies from his garden and place them over the sleeping eyes of someone he thought could use his help. The pansy family knew what they had to do.

Mr. and Mrs. Pansy twisted and turned in their flowerpot until they were able to free themselves from the dirt-root and all. They held on to each other's petals and jumped out of their pots and on to the ground.

They wiggled, and rolled, and shimmied their way into Gina's bedroom. Their children shouted "Hooray!" as they watched their parents lie down over Gina's sleeping eyes.

Friday was unlike any other Friday; it was the day of the snowflake ball and Austin's dad helped him to pick out his clothes for the day.

Gina awoke with Mr. and Mrs. Pansy on her eyes. "That's weird," she thought as she placed the pansies in a cup of water on her nightstand and brought them over to the windowsill to make sure they got plenty of sunlight.

"Hiiiiii Austin," Gina said with heart shaped eyes. Gina had never looked at Austin like that before, it surprised both of them.
"Hey Gina" said Austin. "Do you feel any better?"
"Much better, I'll see you soon!" Gina said.

14

Austin ate a quick breakfast with his family
before going outside to meet Gina.
"Thank you Austin, this is the best get well
soon card ever! okay now open yours."

Austin opened his card and
was completely shocked.
"Will you be my valentine?"
Austin read aloud. "You are
asking ME to be YOUR
VALENTINE?" Austin asked
very puzzled.
"of course Austin, you are my
best friend. so do you want
to go to the snowflake Ball
with me?" Gina asked.

15

"you don't care that people make fun of me?" Austin asked.

"my dad said that people make fun of people they don't understand. I understand you Austin and I think you are great! so do you want to go to the dance with me?"

"of course I do!" Austin said jumping into the air.

They walked to school and had a great time at the snowflake ball.

"We did it!" Exclaimed the pansies. "We helped Gina to get the courage to tell Austin how she really feels!" Even though mr. and mrs. pansy are now living away from their children, they were still able to see their grandchildren bloom from their spot on the windowsill.